BERTA AND ELMER HADER

THO FAR WE MAY ROAM,
THERE'S NO PLACE LIKE HOME.

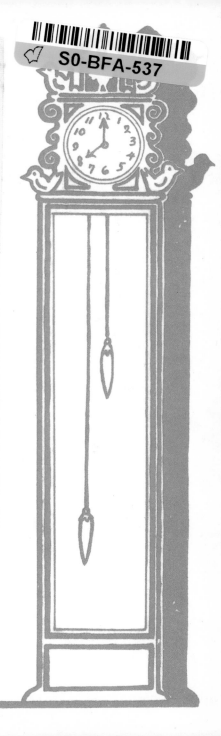

This edition copyright © by Wieser & Wieser, Inc.
and Richard Horner Associates, 1990.

This edition published in 1990 by Gallery Books,
an imprint of W. H. Smith Publishers, Inc.,
112 Madison Avenue, New York, NY 10016.

Gallery Books are available for bulk purchase for sales
promotions and premium use. For details write or telephone
Manager of Special Sales, W. H. Smith Publishers, Inc.,
112 Madison Avenue, New York, NY 10016. (212) 532-6600

Illustrations copyright © by Berta and Elmer Hader, 1927.

ISBN 0-8317-42704

Printed in Hong Kong

WEE WILLIE WINKIE

AND SOME OTHER BOYS AND GIRLS
FROM MOTHER GOOSE

 ILLUSTRATED BY  **BERTA + ELMER HADER**

GALLERY BOOKS

WEE WILLIE WINKIE

Wee Willie Winkie runs through
    the town,
Upstairs and downstairs in his
    nightgown,

Rapping at the window, crying
through the lock,
"Are the children all in bed? For
it's now eight o'clock."

JACK AND JILL

Jack and Jill went up the hill
    To fetch a pail of water;
Jack fell down and broke his crown
    And Jill came tumbling after.

Jack got up and home did trot
    As fast as he could caper;
Went to bed and bound his head
    With vinegar and brown paper.

LITTLE JACK HORNER

Little Jack Horner
Sat in a corner,
Eating of Christmas pie;
   He put in his thumb,
   And pulled out a plum,
And cried, "What a good
   boy am I!"

LITTLE NANCY ETTICOAT

Little Nancy Etticoat,
In a white petticoat;
The longer she stands
The shorter she grows.

MARY HAD A LITTLE LAMB

Mary had a little lamb,
  Its fleece was white as snow;
And everywhere that Mary went
  The lamb was sure to go.

It followed her to school one day.
Which was against the rule;

It made the children laugh and play,
To see a lamb at school.

And so the teacher turned it out,
But still it lingered near;

And waited patiently about
Till Mary did appear.

"Why does the lamb love Mary so?"
The eager children cry;

"Why, Mary loves the lamb, you know!"
The teacher did reply.

JACK

Jack be nimble, Jack be quick,

IMBLE

Jack jump over the candlestick.

LITTLE BO-PEEP

Little Bo-Peep has lost her
  sheep,
And can't tell where to find
  them;
Leave them alone, and they'll
  come home,
Bringing their tails behind them.

Little Bo-Peep fell fast asleep,
    And dreamt she heard them
        bleating;
But when she awoke, she found
    it a joke,
For still they all were fleeting.

Then up she took her little crook,
    Determined for to find them;
She found them indeed, but it
      made her heart bleed,
For they'd left all their tails
      behind 'em.

It happened one day, as Bo-Peep
    did stray
    Into a meadow hard by;
There she espied their tails, side
    by side,
All hung on a tree to dry.

She heaved a sigh, and wiped her
  eye,
    Then went over hill and dale, O!
And tried what she could, as a
  shepherdess should,
    To tack to each sheep its tail, O!

LITTLE TOMMY TUCKER

Little Tommy Tucker
Sings for his supper;
What shall he eat?
White bread and butter;
How will he cut it
Without e'er a knife?
How will he marry
Without e'er a wife?

TOM, THE PIPER'S SON

Tom, he was a piper's son,
He learnt to play when he was young,
But all the tune that he could play
Was "Over the hills and far away."

Tom with his pipe did play with such skill
That those who heard him could never keep still;
As soon as he played they began for to dance,
Even pigs on their hind legs did after him prance.

POLLY PUT THE KETTLE ON

Polly, put the kettle on,
Polly, put the kettle on,
Polly, put the kettle on,
And let's drink tea.

Sukey, take it off again,
Sukey, take it off again,
Sukey, take it off again,
They're all gone away.

THERE WAS A LITTLE GIRL

There was a little girl, and she wore a little curl
Right down the middle of her forehead;
When she was good, she was very, very good,
But when she was bad she was horrid.

One day she went upstairs, while her parents, unawares,
In the kitchen down below were occupied with meals;
And she stood upon her head, on her little truckle-bed,
And she then began hurraying with her heels.

Her mother heard the noise, and thought it was the boys
A-playing at a combat in the attic;
But when she climbed the stair, and saw Jemima there,
She took and she did whip her most emphatic.

LITTLE BOY BLUE

Little Boy Blue, come, blow
   your horn,
The cow's in the meadow, the
   sheep's in the corn;
But where is the little boy tending
   the sheep?
He's under the haycock fast asleep.
Will you wake him?   No, not I!
For if I do, he's sure to cry.

GOOD NIGHT